Michael,
Get end
John Sman

dream a little

D ream

of me

DREAM A LITTLE DREAM OF ME

JOLIE ST. AMANT

Dream a Little Dream of Me

Bienvenue Press, LLC

Youngsville, LA 70592

http://www.bienvenuepress.com

Formatting: CHarmsFormatting

That Voodoo That You Do
"Dream a Little Dream of Me"

This one is dedicated to Colleen. The trips to New Orleans provided so much inspiration for this story! Here's to many more!

Acknowledgments

Thanks goes to my "Boonies", my constant supporters!
Colleen, Val, Denise, Elizabeth, Ruby, Sandy, Melinda,
Tammy, and all of you who comment and keep me writing!
Dennis, thanks for always doing that first read for me.
Gillian, Josh, and Genevieve, thanks for the feedback and the
editing.

My beta readers, Amy and Lisa, you guys rock!

CHAPTER
One

Josey

"*Bienvenue! Welcome to the Chateau Rouge.*"

Mon Dieu, Josey thought as she looked up from the elegant front desk of the New Orleans hotel and fell head over hormones in to lust.

"Checking in," said the object of her affliction. "Name's Rhett. Rhett Butler."

"Rhett Butler?" Josey asked, raising an eyebrow.

An alias, of course. Celebrities often stayed at the *Chateau Rouge* using fake names. She blew a lock of black hair out of her face and hit some keys on the keyboard. Looking up again, she felt a wave of white-hot heat throbbing in the tips of her fangs. Her tongue trailed along the edges, willing them not to show themselves.

His hair was jet black underneath a baseball cap. Tribal tattoos wrapped around arms the size of anacondas. He wore a simple black t-shirt and fashionably tattered blue jeans. His eyes were deep brown, and his five o'clock shadow framed full lips. He was tall—over six feet, by Josey's estimate. He was just her type. Masculine and ragged around the edges. And, somehow, very familiar.

It couldn't be, she thought. *Not after all this time.*

"What can I say? My dad was a *Gone with the Wind* fan," he replied.

"Is that right?"

"Yes, ma'am," he said, leaning over the desk, closer to Josey. "You look like a woman that should be kissed. And often…" His smoky voice trailed off.

"And by someone who knows how," Josey finished for him, breathlessly. She inhaled and stepped back to compose herself before continuing with her normal check-in spiel.

"You are in the Red Light Suite, Mr. Butler. Are you here for the Voodoo Music Experience, or just Halloween in general?"

The Voodoo Music Experience was a rock music festival that attracted people from everywhere. Headliners had been legends like *Ozzy Osbourne* and *KISS*. Of course, haunted New Orleans attracted its fair share of Halloween lovers as well. The French Quarter, decorated in skeletons, ghosts, and ghouls, would be full of costumed revelers.

"I'm here for some kind of experience."

Her eyes met his, and the air between them sizzled. The flame seemed to burn the oxygen out of the air, leaving her lightheaded and half giddy. She sucked in a breath, catching a whiff of

his woodsy cologne. She closed her eyes as the floor seemed to shift.

Only one man had ever made her feel that way. *It couldn't be. Not again.*

She exhaled a breath and choked out, "This key unlocks both your room and the gate to your private courtyard. Enjoy the festival and your stay with us. If you need anything," Josey's voice broke on the word *anything*, "don't be afraid to call the front desk."

Josey held the key out, and Rhett's fingers brushed over hers, moving slowly and deliberately.

Anaconda Arms, aka Rhett Butler, pocketed the key. "If I need any … thing," he winked at her, "you'll be the first one I call, Miss…?"

"Jacobson," she replied. "Josey."

"Josey," he said, then nodded toward the brass plated sign over her shoulder.

"Complimentary happy hour?" he asked.

"Yes. At eight."

"Will you be there?" he asked.

"Maybe," she said.

Damn right I will, she thought. It had been too long since she felt the touch of a man. Too long since she'd fed.

A grin flashed across his face. "I'll see you then."

Josey watched as he disappeared in to the elevator.

"Josey!" Someone was calling her name. "Josey!"

"What?" she snapped.

Ivy, the bartender, was smiling at her from the adjoining door of the hotel's lounge.

"I'm sorry, Ivy," Josey said. "What is it?"

"That was a fine piece of flesh," Ivy teased, raising an eyebrow in the direction of the elevator.

Josey frowned, and started needlessly straightening the top of the Queen Anne desk. "Isn't it time for your shift? What did you do to your hair?" Josey asked Ivy, gesturing to the streak of burgundy in her brown hair.

"I dyed it this morning. Getting all ready for the Vampire Ball this weekend. Do you think Dean will notice?" she asked. Dean was one of the guides for the ghost tour company that used their lounge area as a starting point. He was also Ivy's current beau.

Josey smiled. "If he doesn't, he's blind. It looks good."

3

"Are you coming down for happy hour tonight?"

Josey thought of the man who had just checked in. He was obviously using a fake name. Who was he really? She wouldn't miss happy hour tonight for the world. She had to figure out the mystery man.

"Yes."

"Good. Tobias has been unusually rowdy lately."

"He's probably fussing with Lucy again. You know how they are. I'll come down and keep my eye on things."

"Good. He doesn't listen to me. He almost broke the beer mugs last night."

"Tobias doesn't really listen to anyone. But I'll come down and check it out," Josey said as she turned her attention to the couple walking through the door.

"*Bienvenue!* Welcome to the *Chateau Rouge*," Josey said, and resumed the desk duties.

The night clerk she'd been relieving returned from his break, and Josey checked the time on the slim gold watch on her wrist. Seven o'clock. She had an hour to go to her room, shower, and change. Josey started mentally rifling through her closet. What would she wear?

Josey gave the lobby a last look. Two centuries ago, it had been a bordello, and she, Madame Josephine, had picked every detail from the elaborate crystal chandelier, to the tapestry wall hangings, to the tall white and blue flower arrangements that were delivered from a local florist. Now that it was an upscale boutique hotel, Josey still supervised every detail of the flourishing business. Its reputation as a haunted hotel in New Orleans brought in scores of curious tourists, ghost hunters, and mediums.

Satisfied that everything was as it should be, Josey smiled and headed to her suite.

———

AFTER SHOWERING, Josey donned a soft white robe and stepped out of the bathroom. Her ebony hair was wet and floating around her shoulders. She thought again of Rhett, or whatever his name was. Could it be Archer? Again? Was her mind playing tricks? It had to be. She hadn't fed in some time, and that always messed with her head.

"What do you think we should wear tonight?" she asked, staring in to the walk-in closet.

Silently, a slinky black little dress slid off a hanger and on to the floor. She picked it up.

"No. Not this. Not yet. It's just happy hour," she said. "Something else."

A tight black shirt covered in silvery sequins was next to fall. Josey sighed and put it back.

"Lucy, seriously," she said. "Something less dramatic."

A red sweater slipped off next. One of her favorites. It hugged her curves and showed a slight tease of cleavage. "This is perfect. Thanks, Lucy."

She smiled as she laid the sweater and a pair of slim black slacks on the bed. Before dressing, she had time for a cocktail on the balcony that overlooked the courtyard. She could take in the night sounds and smells, as was her habit, before taking care of business.

She poured a whiskey, neat, and opened the French doors. As she rested her drink on the wrought iron railing, soft music began to play.

Recognizing the melody, she gripped the cold metal. Her glass slipped from her hand and crashed at her feet.

CHAPTER
Two

Archer

RHETT, aka Archer Grayson, surveyed the hotel lounge as he walked in, looking for Josey. The small bar area was decorated much like the rest of the hotel. It was simple, classic, and elegant with a touch of old world New Orleans. Candles flickered in sconces, giving the illusion of gas lighting. Paintings depicting people of generations past flanked the walls in gilded frames.

Along the dark wooden bar, several seats were already taken. There was a couple seated near the end, obviously involved in a spat. They sat staring at their glasses, silent. A mug of beer sat in front of an unoccupied seat.

Archer decided on a seat on the far side of the bar. A little darker, where he could watch the door. One that had an empty seat next to it, for Josey.

"What can I get for you?" the bartender asked.

"Gentleman Jack and water is fine." he said.

She returned with his drink. "You here for the ghost tour?"

"Ghost tour?"

"Yes. One of the local tour groups starts their tours here."

6

She nodded to a group of people in the corner. "They're here for the tour. The hosts should be here soon if you're interested."

Ghosts were the last thing Archer was interested in at the moment. He was looking for something more alive.

He said, "I'll pass tonight."

"They're here every night except Monday if you change your mind," she said, and went to attend to the other customers.

He settled on to his barstool to do one of his favorite things. People watch. Most of the time, the inspiration for his songs came from just sitting and watching. You never knew when an expression or the whisper of a conversation would lead to an idea, and that idea would lead to a lyric, then to a melody.

Suddenly, the volume of soft music that had been unobtrusively drifting through the bar blared, startling the patrons.

The bartender grimaced and grabbed the remote. "Sorry about that, guys. Must have been a power surge or something." As she glared at the empty seat with the beer mug in front of it, the music went up again. Again, the bartender turned the music down with a roll of her eyes.

Archer sipped his drink. Tomorrow night would be sound checks and set lists, and Saturday night, he would perform. In between, he would be scouting the area for undiscovered talent for the record company he was starting. It hadn't been announced officially, but it would be the last tour for him. Too many hours in hotels and on highways.

He tilted his glass to his lips, pausing as Josey walked in. Gorgeous before, she was a knockout in a simple red sweater and black slacks. Her blue eyes scanned the bar. Archer swayed as their eyes met. A flash of a memory of Josey entering the bar wearing a dress from a century ago.

Unsteady, he gulped his drink. The unintentional action caused the whiskey to burn down his throat. He raised his eyes again to hers, and saw a fire raging in her eyes.

Then her eyes widened and she blinked, and the look was gone. She nodded, acknowledging him, before stepping behind the bar. The bartender spoke to her in a low tone, gesturing toward the speakers and the empty seat with the still full mug of beer.

"Ivy?" Josey said, smiling and glancing up at the ceiling. Speaking a little bit louder, she said, "I'm thinking of switching from *Abita* to *Heineken*."

Instantly, the music went silent. She grinned and handed the bartender the remote. "That should do it."

She said something else to the girl, and the bartender turned, looked at him, and frowned. It didn't take a genius to figure out they were talking about him. Archer watched as Josey checked on the still unattended mug of beer. He watched as she poured out the frothy drink and refilled the mug.

Josey fixed herself a drink and made her way from behind the bar to the empty stool beside his. Her perfume drifted up, and his stomach dropped. It was a light, clean, citrusy scent. Nothing flowery or overbearing for her. He also liked the fact that she drank her whiskey neat. She was no fussy, high-maintenance woman.

"Hi again," she said as she sat down.

"Hi there." He nodded toward the bar. "Got the bugs in your system worked out?"

She smiled. "I guess you could say that. These old buildings can be quite … cranky sometimes."

"I'm sure they can."

"So, you said you're here for the Voodoo Festival?" Josey asked.

"That and other business," he said, raising an eyebrow in her direction.

"I've never been," Josey said.

"It's been a while for me."

He had performed there several years ago, just when the band was breaking out. As a favor, they were doing two shows in New Orleans. The first show would be at a smaller, more intimate venue. Later in the week, they would be headlining Voodoo Fest. It seemed like he was coming full circle. He just wished he didn't feel so jaded about the whole thing.

"Halloween is one of our busiest times of the year. My presence is required here."

Archer noted the formal way she spoke with a slight accent. He wanted her to keep talking. The sound was enchanting.

"Maybe I can convince you to go, if only for a little while."

"Maybe so."

"What did you do?" Josey and Archer's attention was drawn to a couple at the bar. The woman was standing next to the guy, with a drink dripping down the middle of her shirt, down her jeans, and on to the floor.

"I didn't do anything!" the guy yelled back. He was awkwardly wiping at the mess with bar napkins.

"You poured your drink on me!"

"I did not!"

"Are you calling me a liar?"

Josey touched Archer's arm, and his pulse spiked at her touch.

"I'll be right back."

Josey approached the woman first. She spoke to the woman quietly, and soon had her calmed down. She walked with her out of the lounge area, then returned to say a few words to the gentleman. Soon, she was back beside Archer, and he was on fire.

He sipped his drink, hoping it would extinguish the flame. He was wrong.

"So, Mr. Butler. What is it you do when you aren't traveling around to music festivals?"

"Pharmaceutical sales," he told her, smiling.

She looked him up and down, noting his tattoos. "I see," she said, and he laughed.

"I'm really in the music business. I'm here scouting out new talent for a record label," he told her.

If she hadn't figured out who he really was yet, he wasn't going to tell her. And maybe she didn't really know. She didn't seem the type to follow the rock music he played. She looked to be more sultry jazz or blues. For now, he wanted to sit and enjoy a drink with a beautiful woman, without the hundred questions he'd heard thousands of times. He'd never been one to flaunt his fame anyway.

"How are you enjoying your stay here at the Chateau so far?" Josey asked.

"Please call me Archer."

She swallowed hard, and her blue eyes turned the color of a darkening sky. Archer had to look away. What he wanted to do at that moment was take her in his arms and push her up against the bar.

She took a sip of her drink. "Archer, that's quite an interesting name. How did you come by it?"

"It's a family name. Has been handed down for generations. In fact, I think one of my predecessors lived here in New Orleans at one time. Maybe that's why I feel such a connection to this town."

Archer watched as she flinched. Before he could ask what was wrong, she smiled at him.

"Speaking of the past, how would you like a grand tour of this place? It has quite a history."

"I think I would like that. Lead on," he said, and finished off his drink.

CHAPTER
Three

JOSEY STOOD ON UNSTEADY FEET. This was a bad, bad idea. Earlier, when her eyes had met his across the bar, memories had flooded her mind. Seeing Archer's disorientation, she knew he had experienced a sense of *déjà vu*. She was playing with fire every moment she spent in his presence.

To steady her nerves, she retreated back in to hotel manager mode and began her tour guide routine.

"This is our lounge area as you can see. In the early days, this is where the bordello's working girls would entertain the customers. They would bring them drinks, listen to their stories, and they would dance. When the Charleston was in fashion, this room would be full of women moving to the music, fringe flying everywhere." Josey resisted the urge to smile as she remembered kicking up her own feet a time or two.

She gestured to the antique piano in the back of the room. "The pianist would play there, and the ladies would crowd around in the middle of the room and dance. In fact, that mirror above the piano? If you snap a picture, every now and then, you can catch images of women in 1920s dresses. Also, customers have reported hearing piano music coming from this room. They come in here to hear more, thinking we have entertainment, only to find no one at the piano, and the music stops."

Now fully composed, she led Archer to the bar corner where the unattended mug of beer sat. "Tobias is rumored to be one of our hotel ghosts. He was our poet and occasional piano player. He was a friend of Tennessee Williams, and they were both known to hang out at *The Hotel Monteleone*. Tobias always came back here because of his affection for one of the dancing girls, Lucy."

Josey picked up the mug. "We keep a mug here for him, as it would seem Tobias has never really left. When Lucy succumbed to the Great Influenza Epidemic in 1918, he was never the same. He passed away in his sleep a little over a year later. Some say he died from a broken heart."

She refreshed the drink. "*The Chateau Rouge* was a brothel until the late 1920s. When new laws came in to effect, we converted to a hotel in the 1930s. The owner and madam, Josephine, my namesake, kept most of the girls on as employees."

She gestured to the lobby area. "Let's go in to the lobby, shall we?"

As Archer walked past her, she caught his scent. She remembered the times she had followed him out of the lounge in the past. She thought of when they would leave and retire to her quarters. She would feed, and they would make love until the sun came up.

Josey swiped her throbbing fangs with her tongue. She still needed to feed. She took a deep breath to steady herself, and pushed the dizziness away.

"When the brothel was converted to a hotel, they didn't

completely redecorate. Some of the original furnishings and features were kept. If you'll look up, you can see images of women in the plaster molding around the chandelier. Personally, I feel like these touches add to the character of the hotel."

She continued to lead him through the hotel, stopping at various rooms to share stories of past guests and those that lingered on after they 'checked-out'. She stopped in front of his room.

"This is your suite, The Red Light Room. This was Lucy's room. Reputedly one of the most haunted rooms in this hotel, other than our lounge. As I shared with you before, Lucy was one of the girls who worked here. Lucy was a romantic, and a matchmaker. Lucy is also said to be one of our ghosts. People have told stories about seeing a woman in an old-style dress sitting on the bed. She smiles, then disappears. She also loves flashy things like jewelry. Items have been known to disappear, then reappear later."

Josey frowned the way she always did when she told stories of Lucy. How she missed her. Even though she was still around, it just wasn't the same.

"Is that right?" Archer asked.

"That's what they say."

"Bet if these walls could talk, they could tell some stories," he said.

"I bet they could," Josey responded.

Hell. Josey could tell them herself. She'd lived them.

Archer slowly closed the distance between them, and her breath caught in her throat. He inched forward, gently pushing until her back was against the hotel room door. He rested his palms on the door behind her, closing her in. She held her breath as he lowered his head. As his lips touched hers, the fire that had been kindling all night long ignited into a slow burn.

His lips moved slowly, and she could taste lingering whiskey. It left her feeling dizzy, almost intoxicated.

With one last, slow kiss, he raised his head. His brown eyes were dark, smoky, and heavy lidded.

"Nice," he said.

Josey's brain was too scrambled to form words or even syllables. She simply nodded.

"Happy hour tomorrow night?" he asked.

She nodded again.

He ran a finger down her arm, and she shivered. He pulled his room key out of his back pocket and reached to open the door.

"I'm going to make you one very happy woman."

CHAPTER
Four

Archer

THE HORSE DRAWN *carriage clapped its way across the brick streets of the old French Quarter. Gas lights flickered on buildings as they passed. The music of the opera they had just attended still played in his mind.*

Josey sat to his right, her full skirt pressing against his leg. A black top hat rested on one knee, her hand on the other. He glanced over at her, and she smiled. He reached down and squeezed her hand gently, then brought it up to his lips, laying a kiss on the soft skin.

ARCHER AWOKE WITH A START. Smelling the sweet scent of floral perfume, he looked around, confused. The room was empty. The aroma quickly faded, and he shook his head. There was nothing but the light from the late afternoon sun filtering in through the French doors.

New Orleans was already doing a number on him. He'd definitely been reading too many history books. It was a favorite hobby of his when he had time. After speaking with the bartender in the lounge the night before, he was considering taking the ghost tour. In other towns he'd visited, the tours usually talked more about the history of the town than actual ghost stories. Being the night owl that he was due to late nights after concerts, they were perfect for him.

He climbed out of bed, slid on boxers, and went to make coffee. He stepped outside on to the balcony to smoke a cigarette while it brewed.

He hadn't paid much attention to the area the night before. A small pool rested in the middle; a fountain was installed in the brick surrounding at one end. Brightly covered pillows rested in the chairs. Pots of palms and tropical flowers were planted at various locations throughout the area. It was a lush oasis surrounded by brick walls.

He looked up at what he knew was Josey's suite. He imagined her lying there, her black hair fanning out against the pillow. Was she naked, like he had just been? Was she thinking of him?

His body responded instantly. He couldn't remember the last time he had been that hot for a woman. It was so instant. So powerful. He needed to have her. Soon.

He stubbed out his cigarette and went back in the room.

———

AFTER COFFEE and one more cigarette, his stomach growled, and he decided to go downstairs to look for food and his other craving, Josey.

It was quiet at the front desk. The day clerk sat reading a book, and he went up to talk to him.

"Reading something good?" he asked the clerk.

His name tag said *Franklin*.

Franklin held up the book. The cover read something

about haunted New Orleans. "It's a new guidebook," he said. "I was checking out what they wrote about us."

"Oh. That's cool. Your boss must be very proud," he said, hoping that would give him some insight as to where Josey might be.

"She hasn't seen it. She hasn't been down yet."

"Is that right?" he asked.

"Miss Josey doesn't come down until later. She's a night owl."

"Oh really?" he asked.

The deep sound of a man clearing his throat made Archer and Franklin turn around. Taller than Archer, and clad in a black suit, the man's dark hair and coloration matched the menace that seemed to surround him. If the man had an aura, it would be black. Archer saw a look of recognition cross the man's face that was quickly veiled.

"Franklin, could you please go and retrieve the daily check-in report for me?"

"Yes, Mr. Alcide," he said, putting the book on the desk and leaving to run the errand.

"Good morning," Alcide said. "Has your stay been pleasant so far?"

Archer thought of last night's encounter with Josey. *If he only knew*, Archer thought. The man's eyes narrowed as if he had read his thoughts. Was he that obvious?

"It has, so far."

"And just how long will you be staying with us, Mr...?"

Archer had the feeling that the imposing man did not like him. Must not be a rock fan. Archer wasn't one to judge, but the way the guy was dressed and the way he carried himself, Archer thought he was probably in to more classical music than heavy metal.

"For the week. Until Voodoo Fest is over," Archer said.

The tall man frowned. "If you find you need anything during your short stay here with us, please feel free to contact me. My name is Alcide Santiago. I am the day manager as well as head of security."

Alcide's dark eyes met Archer's. "I ensure that there are no problems for Ms. Jacobson."

Archer had the suspicion that Santiago was including him in the 'problems', but had no idea why.

"Good evening, Mr…" Alcide said, prompting Archer for his name again.

"Butler," Archer said, sticking to his alias.

"Right," Alcide said, raising one dark brow. "Mr. Butler. Again, enjoy your stay."

Alcide nodded and left the front desk, disappearing in to an elevator.

"Is there anything else I can help you with?" the desk clerk said as he returned.

Archer checked his watch. He had enough time to venture out for a meal and a walk through the Quarter before happy hour. "I'm good."

He'd have to wait to see Josey.

Eight o'clock couldn't come fast enough.

———

Josey

JOSEY WOKE WITH A START. She had been dreaming of Archer; of that night in the carriage after the opera. That had been one of their last nights together before he died the first time. She looked at her hand, almost still able to feel his warm fingers in her cold hand.

She smelled coffee brewing. The dark chicory kind that

was popular only in the South.

It was a vice she had not given up since she was mortal. That was over two hundred years ago.

"Josephine."

The deep voice across the room could be none other than Alcide. No one else would dare enter her room while she was sleeping. They would have to get past him first. And if they did, waking Josey could mean ending up as a midnight snack. Or worse.

"You've seen him, haven't you?" she said.

"Yes. *Ma chere'*, I knew he was here. I felt your reaction."

She exhaled and threw the covers off the bed. She was naked, but it was nothing Alcide hadn't seen before. He had been with her since her making. Her protector, confidante, and friend.

She drew on her robe and crossed to the French doors, opening them to let in the humid New Orleans air. Even after all this time, she still preferred fresh air over the filtered and chilled air conditioning. Especially in the evening. She loved the sounds and smells of the New Orleans nights.

She stood on the balcony, and looked down toward Archer's room. In one former life, he'd been a riverboat gambler, in the *Chateau Rouge* for some company and entertainment. In another, he'd been a bootlegger, providing the Rouge with the liquor banned by Prohibition. She had loved him fiercely, and lost him twice. Both times, she'd been too late to save him. He'd drowned in a steamboat accident, and then shot in a sale gone bad. He had lost too much blood by the time she got there to save him or turn him.

"What are we going to do?" Alcide asked, crossing over to the balcony to join her. His footsteps were silent as if he glided rather than walked. A feat for such a massive man.

"He doesn't remember me. He doesn't remember anything about the past. I think he saw a flash last night at the bar. He is a regular mortal, with regular thoughts, memories, and dreams. Like he's always been."

"He's leaving in a few days," Alcide said. "You can always just let him go."

Josey felt the jab in her heart like a stake.

"What's going to be worse? Letting him go and live, or watching him die again?"

As her protector, he was linked to her feelings. He may not have been able to read her thoughts, but he knew when she was hurt, physically or emotionally. The Voodoo Queen who made Josey into a vampire after she had taken ill from yellow fever had bound them together. when she'd made the two of them. He had felt her pain just as she had when Archer died.

Alcide continued, "You can let him go now, or let history repeat itself. You can fall in love with him all over again and watch him die. Again."

"Who says he has to die this time?"

"Who says he won't?"

Josey felt a soft rustle across her legs. "Hello there, Spook."

She picked up the grey cat and stroked its fur while continuing to look out at the lights across the courtyard.

"You're right, of course, my friend. In a week, he can go about his business and finish out his life. It would be easier that way. For both of us."

"Of course I'm right." His lips curved in a rare smile. "It's my job to be right."

Josey nodded. "All I have to do is stay out of his way. Alcide, you will see to the hotel? I will make myself scarce. No accidental run-ins."

"Of course, *ma chère*," he said with a deep bow. "Now, I will go tend to the business. I will be here if you need me."

She smiled at him. "Thank you, old friend."

"My pleasure. I will see that you feed soon, too. I feel your hunger."

"Thank you."

The door opened and closed as Alcide exited. Josey continued to gaze out across the courtyard.

"It's not right, Miss Josey."

Josey looked over to the new voice in the room. Lucy had materialized, and was sitting on the edge of her bed. She was still dressed as she would have been when she was one of the most popular prostitutes of the *Chateau Rouge*. Her scarlet red dress fanned out around her. Red and black feathers adorned her long brown hair.

"Lucy, it's the right thing to do."

"But what if it's different this time?" she asked, always the hopeless romantic.

"What if it's not? What if it's like Alcide says and I have to lose him all over again? I can't do it. I won't do it."

"But…" Lucy started.

Josey cut her off with a smile. "Now, Lucy, don't be meddling in my love life. It's not something you can fix. Not like that couple from Savannah that just checked in."

"Ms. Josey, they're so sad," Lucy said, frowning. "They look at each other, so full of longing, when they think the other isn't looking. I started working on them right away. I still have some more tricks up my sleeve. And I can go see Miss Vivian. They'll walk out of here hand in hand. I promise."

"Good girl," Josey said. "Now, why don't you go work your magic, or go see to Tobias? He's been missing you lately."

"I will, Miss Josey." She glided over to Josey. "And think about making things right with Mr. Rhett. As they always say, third time's a charm."

"Yeah, or the third time will kill you," Josey said. Her attention was drawn to the room across the courtyard where a light came on. Archer was back.

She longed to go to him. To hear his voice. To feel his touch. To feel the press of his body against hers. Just one more time.

She took one last look across the courtyard and closed the door.

Alcide

ALCIDE SANTIAGO DUCKED his tall frame through the door of *Enchantée*, an antique store on Royal Street in the French Quarter. A bell chimed as the door opened, and an old woman with skin the color of cafe au' lait stood behind the counter.

He lowered his head for a moment in respect. "Madame Vivian, how do you fare today?"

"Alcide, *mon cher*. I am well." Her blue eyes surveyed him. "Better than you, I see."

"I am worried about Josephine."

"He has returned?"

Alcide nodded.

"I have suspected that he would."

She gestured to the array of tarot cards laid out on her counter. She tapped a worn card with a big wheel illustrated on it.

"What do you see?"

"The decision will ultimately be hers, as it always has

been. The cycle will continue one way or another. Such is life. The wheel has already begun to turn, my friend."

Alcide exhaled a heavy breath.

"You will continue to be there as always, the faithful friend, though I hope this time it works out for the best. For you both."

"Thank you, Madame Vivian. I need to return to my duties. If you will excuse me."

"Of course."

Heart heavy, Alcide nodded once more and left the store.

CHAPTER
Five

Archer

ARCHER FOUND a restaurant overlooking Jackson Square. The place had huge doors that opened out on to the brick walkway, allowing the fall breeze to blow in and flutter the flames of the candles on each table. He watched tarot card readers and artists sell their wares, along with the homeless people that wandered about, some occupying the metal benches surrounding the square.

Halloween in New Orleans, Archer thought. One of the most haunted places in the country, and he was staying in a hotel that advertised it had ghosts. No wonder he was having weird dreams. He'd already walked through the Quarter, admiring its decorations. Every business on Bourbon Street had some kind of ghost, goblin, or witch towering above and looking down at you. Add that to the various voodoo shops, and you had a recipe for creepy.

The waiter brought him the classic New Orleans dish. Red beans and rice. The spicy smell wafted up, and Archer felt lightheaded. He'd eaten that dish before. The flash of a memory of a china bowl filled with red beans and rice, the sounds of piano music, and the tinkle of women's laughter skirted through his mind.

He shook his head and took a drink of whiskey.

The town was definitely starting to get to him.

―――――

AFTER FINISHING DINNER, Archer meandered through the Quarter, still feeling strange. Everything looked familiar, like home. Even hearing his boots pound against the brick seemed like a sound he'd heard before. Yes, he'd visited a time or two before in the past, doing shows, but he'd never really taken the time to really explore New Orleans. Back then, it had been get to town, check in, party, play, repeat. He'd never walked through the other streets. Never peered in the windows of the stores.

His wanderings took him down Royal Street and the many antique shops lining it. He stopped and looked in a few windows, marveling at the decadence in the stores. Sparkling chandeliers, statues of lions, and gilded pieces of furniture were displayed like the jewels they were.

Suddenly, Archer stopped cold, startling the people walking behind him.

The word *Enchantée* was scrolled in white on the glass storefront. That store was different than the ones he'd seen before. It wasn't full of furnishings and decorations. The display area in front showed off jewelry, antique cameras, photos, and other items most people would consider personal. It was the phonograph that caught his attention.

He pulled open the door, and a bell tinkled in welcome.

A woman as old as some of the wares inside came out from behind a curtain of beads. A smile warmed her leathery face, and her sparkling blue eyes belied her age.

"Welcome to *Enchantée*. Is there somethin' I can help you with, *mon cher*?" Her voice had a slight French accent that reminded him of Josey's. *Josey*, he thought. His body reacted the way it always did when he thought of her.

"I see," the old woman said.

She eyed him, and Archer resisted the urge to shiver. It felt like she looked right through his soul.

He shook off the sudden chill and gestured to the antique record player in the window. "That Victrola, it's for sale?"

"You don't want dat old thing, *cher*."

Archer smiled. The old lady wasn't much of a salesperson.

"Why not?"

"It don't work."

"Surely it just needs some work."

"Dat won't help."

"You've tried to have it fixed?"

Archer didn't care if it worked or not. He wanted it.

"No, *cher*."

"How much will you take for it?"

"It's not for sale." She gestured to a stool across from her. "Have a seat. Let Ms. Vivian tell you a story."

Archer wasn't really in the mood for a story, but he sat anyway. *This should be interesting at least*, he thought.

She shuffled around the counter and went and grabbed the Victrola. She sat it in front of Archer, looking deep in to his eyes as she did. Archer got the feeling she was looking for something, but wasn't sure what.

She ran a hand lovingly over the brass horn speaker before she began to speak. "All of these items in the store, they have a story. Some stories are tragic, some are happy, but they all have tales to tell. This particular piece was bought by a young bootlegger in the 1920s. He bought it for a young madam at one of the bordellos in the French Quarter.

"See, this young madam loved music and loved to dance. There were times her and her girls would dance up a storm for the customers. The Charleston had just come in to fashion, you see. And they loved the fancy, fast steps. When the young man happened upon this Victrola, he knew he had to buy it for his lover. He put it in his fancy new automobile and left out on a run, looking forward to seeing the look in her eyes when he gave it to her.

"He was ambushed on the road. The robbers took his stash of alcohol—it was priceless back in those days—and left him by the side of the road, bleeding out from a gunshot wound. When all was said and done, his body laid to rest, this old Victrola was delivered to his lover's door.

"In her grief, the young woman vowed she would never listen to the record player. 'I vow that music never plays from this machine until I hear my lover's heartbeat again'."

"She ordered it packed up and brought here to *Enchantée*. But, the old lady who owned the store never sold it. The curse stuck, and this old thing has never played one note of music. And here it still sits."

"So, you don't really know if it works or not?" Archer asked.

She smacked his hand. "How dare you question an old woman. I said it don' work, it don' work."

Archer smiled, admiring the old lady's spunk.

The door chimed again, and a couple came in to the store.

"I'll tell you what, boy. So you don't leave here with nothin', I want you to come back soon and let Madame Vivian read your cards for you."

He nodded. He would definitely be back. He wasn't taking no for an answer on the Victrola.

"Yes, *cher*. I will see you soon."

Those blue eyes of hers bored in to his, and Archer felt the chill all the way to his bones.

"Good day," she said, and Archer bowed his head.

"Goodbye, Madame Vivian. Until next time."

He shivered as a cold wind blew through him as he exited the store.

...

At 7:30, Archer entered the lounge. Yes, he was early, but he was also thirsty. The day had been weird. It had all started with that dream, the feeling he'd had at dinner, and then the visit with the eccentric Madame Vivian. The head of security had frowned at him as he walked through the lounge on the way to the bar. Archer still had no idea why the man seemed to detest him.

"Bourbon and Coke," he said as the same bartender who had been there the night before approached him.

She smiled. "Sure thing."

She returned quickly and set the drink in front of him. "You're him, aren't you?"

"Him?" He raised an eyebrow.

"Archer Grayson. Lead singer of *Epiphany*."

Archer thought of lying for a moment, of saying they just looked similar, like he usually did. But the way the young woman raised a brow of her own, as if she knew what he was thinking, had him nodding. *Jesus*, he thought. *Why does it seem like everyone reads minds in New Orleans?*

The bartender's grin was a quick flash of white teeth.

"You've had an interesting day here in New Orleans today?"

"Yes," he admitted. "Interesting is a good word for today."

She smiled again. "I'm a big fan, by the way. I have all

your albums. It's awesome to meet you after all this time. I'm Ivy," she said, holding out a hand.

As he shook her hand, he noted how cold she was. He looked up, and she must have seen the question in his eyes.

"My hands are always cold. I'm anemic." She grinned again.

The volume on the music shot up. "Excuse me," Ivy said. Archer watched as she lowered the sound, and refilled the ever-present beer mug on the corner.

Archer sipped his drink, looking up every time someone walked in to the lounge. He was like a kid with a crush.

He drank, and watched the minute hand as it clicked by. Eight o'clock passed by with no Josey. Thinking she must have gotten caught up with work, he didn't worry too much. He thought about the night before, of kissing her, of what he was going to do with her later that evening.

His body reacted the way it did when he thought of her, and he turned his thoughts somewhere else, so as not to embarrass himself in public.

Eight thirty.

"Would you like another?" the bartender asked when he finished off his drink.

"Yes. I would. And can you tell me if Ms. Jacobson will be attending happy hour tonight?"

He hated to ask, but found he couldn't help himself. He had to know where she was.

"Oh. No, Mr. Grayson. We got notice from Mr. Santiago today. Ms. Jacobson is indisposed and not to be bothered. We are to go to him if we need anything."

"Is that right?"

"Yes."

Archer downed the rest of the drink and set the glass on the bar. "We'll just see about that, won't we?"

Ivy's eyes widened slightly, then she grinned again. "Careful, Mr. Grayson. What's that old cliché? You might be biting off more than you can chew."

"We'll just see who's biting," he said.

Her lips twitched as if she was holding back laughter. As he turned to walk away, he heard her mutter, "Yes. We will, won't we?"

CHAPTER
Six

Josey

JOSEY WATCHED the time tick away on the antique clock in her living room. She held a TV remote in one hand and a drink in the other. The drink and her hunger were making her light-headed. In her ravenous condition, Archer would be in trouble. Her raging hormones and appetite would have him against the wall, fangs buried deep in that pulsing vein in his neck. His blood would taste like home.

He had known what she was in his other lives. She hadn't been able to keep it from him. How else could she have explained that she could never eat with him before sundown? Or stay with him when the sun came up if she wasn't in a place no light could penetrate?

How could she have explained the fangs? Or that she needed blood to survive? She could exist on mortal food, but it weakened her. Surely, Alcide would come soon. He would come, and they would go out on Bourbon Street and find a willing participant. They would go to one of those 'vampire' bars. She wasn't the only one of her kind in New Orleans. A few enterprising vamps had taken advantage of the town's lore and opened places tourists and wannabe blood suckers flocked to. A buffet for the undead. She would feed and erase any memory that she'd been there. She'd leave the person feeling like they had drunk too much the night before. Not unusual for people carousing on Bourbon. Any memory of her would be hazy, like a veiled curtain. Most would think it was all a dream brought on by absinthe, that Green Fairy, and the overall mystique of the French Quarter.

There was a knock on her door. She frowned. Alcide never knocked, and would have taken care of any situations that may have arisen in the hotel.

Must be an employee that didn't get the memo.

She opened the door, and her heart stopped. It was Archer.

"What are you doing here?"

"I went down for happy hour," he said. "You weren't there."

"You shouldn't be here, Archer."

He stepped closer, and as he approached, she could hear the blood thundering in his veins. She took a step back. To protect herself or him, she wasn't sure.

Undeterred, he kept coming.

"You need to go," she said, her voice ragged.

"Why?"

"I don't want you here," she lied.

He reached out; his guitar hardened thumb rubbed her cheek.

"Liar," he whispered, his voice husky.

Thump, thump, thump. The beating of his heart was like the rhythm of one of his rock songs. Strong and hard. She closed her eyes against the sound. Archer took that as a sign of her submission and leaned in. His lips brushed hers. His hand still on her cheek.

33

The press of his lips against hers threatened her resolve. If he knew how dangerous his position was, he would run screaming for the door. Or not. He never had before. In the past, he had always enjoyed walking the line, knowing his life was in her hands. He loved living life on the edge. The rush of adrenaline quickened him, and her as a result. He was always aware that with a flick of her wrist or an ounce of blood too much, his life as he knew it would be over. Once, he had even begged for her to turn him. She had not. For as much as she loved him, turning him, and tearing him from the sheer enjoyment of being a mortal, was unthinkable. He didn't remember any of that, but Josey did, and the memory of the pain of his loss restored her control. She put her palms on his chest and pushed.

"Go. Now!"

"Tell me you don't want this as badly as I do and I will."

Oh, but she did. She wanted it. And more. She wanted to push him against the wall like he had done to her the night before. She wanted to wad that shirt in her fists and pull it over his head. Run her fingers down that warm chest.

Her brain scrambled as his other hand snaked under her shirt, and his fingers tickled her ribcage. His hand froze upon feeling her cold skin, as if realizing she wasn't normal.

Panic seized her as she felt her fangs lengthen. She couldn't hold back much longer. He was too close to learning the truth.

Her hands still pressed against his chest, she pushed him firmly backward. She told herself to breathe.

Her door opened, and she felt Alcide's dark presence.

"Is there a problem here?" he asked.

Archer stiffened and took a protective stance in front of

Josey. She stepped up when she saw the defiant look in Archer's eyes.

Knowing how deadly that could be for him, Josey responded, "No. Archer was just leaving."

Archer's dark eyes met hers, as if extending a challenge.

"For now," he said.

"Josephine, you remember we have plans for this evening," Alcide said.

"Of course," Josey said. "It's time."

Archer looked at them both. "We'll continue this later," he said to Josey

"We shall see about that," Alcide said.

"Alcide," Josey said, "give me a moment to grab my coat."

Archer stared at her a moment longer, then nodded.

"This isn't over," he said.

Josey took a deep breath as he walked out of the door. She leaned against the bar for a moment to compose herself.

When she had regained control, she said, "Let's get this over with."

Alcide offered his arm, and just like she had so many times in the past, she took it.

"He's following us, *ma cherie*," Alcide said as they walked through the lobby of the hotel.

"I know," Josey said.

"We will have to lose him. He cannot go where we are going. It's dangerous for him. And, more importantly, a distraction for you."

"We will as soon as we get in to the crowd."

"We will meet at the normal location?" he asked.

"Of course."

"I will see you there," Alcide said.

As soon as they stepped in to the crowd, they separated,

each moving so fast, the people around them merely felt the breeze. The more psychically aware person felt the menace along with the wind, and would look around in fear but see nothing.

Josey ducked in to the entrance of the vampire bar. Most people avoided the wooden door under the old-fashioned sign in the shape of a battle axe. Instantly, she felt eyes drawn to her. Number one: she was a female entering a vampire bar. Number two: she was stunningly beautiful. A gorgeous woman entering such an establishment was either brave or borderline suicidal.

She nodded in greeting to a few of the others there like her. For protection, they never gathered in friendly groups in public. Better to draw as little attention to themselves as possible. They were known, however, to gather in private parties. Those parties were the things movies were made of.

In the dark bar, a few had already claimed some foolish humans. Blood lust ran through the air like an electrical current that could be felt even by some more perceptive humans. A feeling of danger, coppery and warm, mixed with the heavy metal music playing from the speakers. The place was not for the faint of heart.

Josey stood a head taller than most men, having been chosen by her maker for her height. The six-inch heels on her black leather boots made her tower over many people in the bar in general. Her icy blue stare only intensified the feeling of intimidation, and by the time she had made her way to the bar, several men had decided to give her a wide berth. A willing participant would be hard to find that evening. Her hunger hummed through her body. She slid on to an empty barstool, and the bartender, also a vampire, nodded and slid her a whiskey, straight up.

"You dining with us this evening?" the vamp asked.

"I am."

"Well, take a look at our menu." The vamp smiled "If you see anything you like, let me know."

"I will," Josey said.

She looked at her watch. Where was Alcide? They should have arrived almost exactly at the same time. She wouldn't feed without him. Feeding took all her attention, and she needed someone to watch her back. New Orleans wasn't safe on a general basis, and the alleyway behind the bar even less so. She wasn't scared of what a human could do, but with modern investigations and DNA analysis, messes with humans were complications no vampire needed.

Josey took the glass and turned around to survey the bar and the humans writhing to the beat of the hard rock music pounding through the space. What was she in the mood for tonight?

Definitely something tall, dark, and handsome. Someone she could close her eyes and pretend was Archer. Maybe she should go with something short and blond so that there would be no temptation. No. Short would never do for her. She already felt like a brute when feeding. To tower over someone would make it feel even worse. She continued her survey of the bar, still wondering where Alcide was.

Alcide

ALCIDE SLID in to stride with Archer, who was walking through the Quarter, thinking he could catch up with the two of them.

"Enjoying your stroll through our beautiful Quarter this fine evening?" Alcide asked Archer.

Archer started in surprise, but hid it quickly. "What do you think?"

"Is there anything in our town that I can help you find?"

"Somehow, I don't think you'll help me with what I'm looking for right now."

"You would be better off if you left well enough alone. Trust me. Walk away and don't look back," Alcide said.

"And if I don't?"

In two hundred years and three different lifetimes, the human had not changed. He was still impossibly stubborn and determined. Alcide resisted the urge to shake his head. Some mortals never learned.

———

Josey

JOSEY FELT Alcide's presence beside her before she turned to him.

"You're late," she said.

"Yes. I had some business to attend to."

Josey knew what 'business' he was referring to. There was only one thing that would keep him from joining her.

"Leave Archer alone."

"Oh. I have no intention of harming that man, unless, of course, I need to."

Josey's blue eyes scanned the bar again, looking for a willing participant. In the dark corner across from them, a lone male gave her the eye. He was exactly what she was looking for, and he had that reckless gleam in his eye that told her he would be up for a romp in the alleyway. His audacity reminded her of Archer.

She felt that familiar pang, and she flinched. She would be stronger after she fed. Emotionally as well as physically.

"You desire that one?" Alcide asked.

"Yes."

"Go, then. I will wait."

Josey took a final sip of her drink and set it on the bar. She pasted a smile on her face, careful to hide her fangs as always, and made her way to her prey in the corner, never taking her eyes off his. Already weaving him in to her spell.

"Hi," he said as she reached him.

"Hi."

"Get you a drink?"

"That, or we could skip all that and take a walk outside," she said. She wasn't in the mood for small talk, and her hunger had become painful, leaving her nerves tingling and her senses dulled. She needed to feed. Now.

He smiled and set his drink down on the bar.

"Follow me," she said.

Josey led the nameless piece of meat to a dark place in the alley. There were others there, feeding like she was about to. There were pairs of people and the occasional threesome, tucked in to the shadows of corners and alcoves. A restaurant for the damned.

She led him away from the prying eyes of others in to one of the dark doorways of a business that had been closed since Katrina. There would be no interruptions. Alcide would see to that.

When she pushed him against the door, he had no problem letting her take the lead.

Playing along, Josey let him place a few kisses on her neck, behind her ear.

Feeling weak with hunger, she laid a few kisses on his jawbone, and ran her fingers through his hair, giving him an illusion of passion. Her palm slid down to one side of his neck, and her lips teased the other. Fangs elongated, she bit in to the soft skin of his neck.

He stiffened, and she strengthened her grip on his neck. She drank from him, feeling the healing power of the dark liquid burn down her throat, like the bourbon she favored.

As she drank, she thought of Archer. Of how he had allowed her to drink from him in the past. Had begged her to. The passion that they felt when she was finished had made them both crazy.

Her body reacted instantly, and she broke the bond. She licked the wound she had inflicted and took a step back. Pretended to straighten her clothes.

The guy looked at her through a hazy fog.

"You were amazing," she said, giving him one final kiss.

She looked him in eye and did her mind trick. Mr. Nameless walked away, thinking he had just gotten the night of his life in the shadows. Josey knew he'd probably come back to the same bar the next night and look for her, wondering if she had been a figment of his imagination and wanting more. But she would not be there.

For now, she was satisfied.

Alcide

ALCIDE WATCHED as Josey's color, what little she had, returned. She had almost waited too long. Feeding had always been a necessary evil for her, only to be done when needed. Unless Archer was in her life. She had always been well satisfied when he was there. And the more nourished she was, the more powerful she was.

"Better?" he asked her.

"Much," she said. "I'll be returning to my room now. You will continue to take care of the hotel?"

"Of course, *ma chère*."

"A few more days."

"Yes. You can do this."

"It will be different this time."

"Yes."

And with that, Josey was gone.

Alcide squared his shoulders and pulled the sleeves down on his suit jacket. He reached inside his breast pocket and pulled out a dark clove cigarette and lit it. Walking down the brick sidewalks of the dark New Orleans alley, the echo of his Italian leather shoes was the only sound.

CHAPTER
Seven

Archer

ARCHER ROAMED through the crowded streets alone, ignoring the texts from his bandmates, who had arrived that day. They wanted to meet for drinks and enjoy all the pleasures the Quarter had to offer. There was only one pleasure he wanted, and she was nowhere to be found. What had happened between last night and now?

Where could she have gone? Why was her security guard so intent on keeping them apart? Did the guy have a thing for Josey himself? Archer wondered. He took a final look around the streets and shook his head in frustration. It was useless. If someone didn't want to be found on Bourbon, it was almost impossible to locate them.

He ducked in to a quiet bar and took a stool. He ordered his usual, and was sipping it silently when he felt a pain in his neck, like a bite. Dizziness clouded his mind as he looked around. No one was near. He imagined the black hair he'd seen in his dreams in front of him, those shiny locks trailing down his chest, her hand on his neck, holding him in place. He couldn't see her face, but, somehow, she and that feeling was familiar.

He shook his head and downed his drink to try to clear his mind. New Orleans was definitely doing weird things to his head. It was time to call it a night. Before he went to his room, he would stop in at the bar. Just in case Josey had changed her mind.

———

Alcide

"I KNOW YOU'RE THERE, LUCY," Alcide said as he pulled off his coat to hang it in the closet. When he turned, she had materialized and was sitting on the edge of his bed. The bright red of her dress was a striking contrast against the black duvet. He walked over to the bar and poured himself a drink.

Leaning against the minibar, he took a sip and waited, one eyebrow raised, waiting for what he knew was coming.

"This isn't right, Mr. Alcide. Fate isn't something you can fight. Those two are meant to be together, and you know it. Why do you think he keeps coming back?"

"Pray, tell me, why he keeps dying? Why does he have to keep coming back in the first place?"

She exhaled a deep breath of ghostly air, and the very air in the room dropped in temperature.

Unfazed, Alcide met her stare. Frustrated, she got up from the bed and began pacing the room.

"We have to do something this time. What if we changed something?"

"Changed what?"

"I don't know, but we have to do something. Think about it. What if he stays? What if you could finally be released, Alcide? Don't you think

43

you've protected her long enough? For two hundred years, I've watched you. No happiness, no love. Nothing but serving Josey. Don't you get tired, Alcide? This could be your chance, too."

Phantom pain sliced through his nonexistent heart.

"Enough! Two times I've lived through this with Josey. She almost died the last time. As did I."

"So that's it? You're scared? I wouldn't have thought that of you."

Anger flashed through him. "Careful, Lucy. You tread in dangerous waters." His sharp voice cut through the cold air in the room.

"What are you going to do to me?" She strode over to him, her icy finger poking in to his chest. She moved closer to him. "If you aren't going to do something, I will."

And with that closing statement, she disappeared.

"Damn it!"

Alcide poured himself another drink, downed it, then stormed out of his room. He needed to be downstairs for any chaos Lucy intended to create.

———

Archer

"THAT KIND OF DAY, HUH?" Ivy asked as she poured Archer another drink.

The bar was empty except for the couple that had been there the first night he had come in. Romantic New Orleans had not worked its magic on those two if their silence indicated anything. Both sat staring at their drinks, barely speaking. Archer did note the way they looked at each other when they thought the other wasn't looking. If he was in a better mood, he would have penned some lyrics on a bar napkin.

Archer said nothing in response to Ivy. Just stared down at his own glass. Ivy poured herself a glass of red wine and walked around the bar to sit beside him.

"Want to talk about it?"

"Aren't you working?" His voice was sharper than he intended, but it didn't seem to faze her.

"What work? Those two over there aren't talking. And they're barely drinking."

"What would your boss say if she came down here and saw you drinking with the customers?"

She grinned. "It wouldn't be the first time."

Again, Archer got the feeling that she was laughing at some inside joke that he just didn't get.

The faulty sound system chose to act up again at that moment. The air in the room suddenly chilled, and Ivy's grin fell into a frown. The old classic '*Dream a Little Dream of Me*' started playing. Ella Fitzgerald's throaty voice blended in with trumpets and *Louis Armstrong*'s unique sound.

As the first notes drifted out of the speakers, Archer's body went cold. Dizzy, he brought his hands up to his temples.

The woman in white flashed in front of his eyes again. Bright red lips curved into a sultry smile that welcomed him. He closed his eyes, trying to shake the hazy vision. That only made it worse. The image became more solid, the scent of jasmine playing across his face. If only he could see the face. As he tried, his head began to pound. He flinched against the pain. The headaches that had started plaguing him before his arrival in New Orleans were getting worse.

"Are you okay?"

He exhaled a shaky breath. "I'm okay."

She narrowed her dark eyes at him for a moment. She took another sip of the wine. "If you'll excuse me."

"Call me Archer, please," he said, and the whisper of a flinch crossed her face.

She blinked once before responding. "Archer, then. I'll return shortly."

She crossed back behind the bar, hit a button on the remote, and changed the song. She picked up the phone and spoke softly.

Within moments, Alcide Santiago's forbidding frame was crossing the bar.

"I'm sorry to bother you, Alcide, but there seems to be a problem with our sound system again." She paused for a moment and raised an eyebrow. "As well as the thermostat."

"It's no problem. I was already on my way here. I was afraid this would happen this evening." He frowned at the mug on the corner of the bar, then turned his eyes to the ceiling. His lips were tight with disapproval.

"How's Josey?" Ivy asked softly.

Archer strained to hear the response. What was going on?

"Better. But restless. You know how she is after one of our nights out."

"I wish she wouldn't wait so long. It's not good for her."

Alcide nodded. "I know."

The volume on the music spiked again, and the same song started as before. As the brassy sound of the trumpet rang out in the bar, Archer felt himself sway. Again, he saw the image of black hair. He felt cold hands on his chest, and long teeth scraping the side of his neck.

He took another drink to steady his nerves, hoping the whiskey would shake him out of whatever was going on with him.

"I can't fix this problem in here. This requires a more

personal touch," Alcide said to Ivy. "Do what you can until I return. Keep an eye on our man over there. He has more brawn than brains sometimes."

Archer looked around the bar. Did they mean him? They had to. He scowled at Alcide's retreating figure. The man really was too much. He set his drink down on the bar.

"You want another?"

"No. I think I've had quite enough for now. You can send the bill to my room. Good luck with the bugs in your system tonight."

As he walked by the couple at the bar, he heard his name whispered to Ivy. He had been recognized. To her credit, she didn't blow his cover.

She said, "We get a lot of people in here. Some are famous. Some just look like celebrities."

Archer would have to get some tickets for them and for Ivy. Those two looked like they needed some fun, and Ivy, because she looked like she would enjoy the show. She didn't get all star struck either.

There was only one woman he wanted fawning all over him. And she was doing her best to avoid him. As the elevator doors closed, instead of hitting the button to take him to his room, he pressed the one for Josey's floor.

He rapped on her door and waited for a response. Nothing. He knocked again, a little louder. Still nothing. After a third try, he sighed heavily and headed to his own room.

His thoughts were still on Josey as he slid the door open.

A cool wind blew through the room, and on the breeze, the scent of jasmine.

Josey, he thought.

He looked around his room, but there was no one there. In the middle of his bed lay an ornate, antique key. He went over and picked it up. It was a skeleton key used in old houses. In the middle of the curved metal lay a heart-shape. A red ribbon was attached to it as a makeshift keychain.

"What the hell?" Archer asked.

He felt the cool breeze drift through the room again, and on it, he could smell the scent of flowers. In the quiet of the room, he could almost imagine hearing soft footsteps cross the carpet and the whisper of satin.

He went through the suite, looking for anything else that might be amiss. It wouldn't be the first time a crazy fan had bribed a maid to sneak in to his room. Everything seemed to be as it should be. So where had the key come from? And where could he find out? He couldn't ask the head of security. Who would know where a key that unique would belong? Ivy the bartender? She definitely seemed to know a lot more than she let on. But she wouldn't be forthcoming with any information that Alcide didn't want known.

He jumped at a knock on the door.

"Josey?" he asked as he opened the door.

There was no one there. There was no one in the hallway.

"What the hell is going on?" he whispered.

At the end of the hall, the elevator opened. Still, there was not a soul around. Instead of closing, the silver doors stayed open, as if waiting.

Unable to resist the mystery, he grabbed his own room key, slid it in to his pocket, and went to the elevator. When he stepped in, the button labeled 'R' lit up. He pressed it and the doors swooshed closed.

The elevator opened, and he stepped out on to the roof. A brick fence stood high enough to provide privacy and security to whomever might be enjoying the area just beyond.

A black, wrought iron gate separated him from whatever was on the roof. He looked at the key in his hand. With a shrug of his shoulders, he took the key and slid it in to the lock. It fit. He turned it, and then tried the latch. The gate opened. Again, the scent of flowers.

He stepped in to a hidden oasis. Green palm trees were lit with tiny white lights. Night blooming flowers, like jasmine, filled the air with their sweet scent. The walls were high and covered in thick ivy. A pool glistened in the middle of it all like an emerald. Wisps of steam rose up in the cool fall air.

Floating in the water on her back was Josey, and she was looking up at the stars. Drawn to her, he walked to the edge of the pool.

"You shouldn't be here, Archer," she said without looking at him.

"You keep saying that," he said, kicking his shoes off.

"You don't know what you're getting in to."

"Tell me, then." He slid his shirt off and laid it on the wrought iron table next to him.

"It's a long story."

"I've got nothing but time." He unbuttoned his jeans and slid them to the ground.

His belt buckle clinked on to the tile. Josey stopped floating then and swam to the edge of the pool.

In the moonlight, her eyes were brighter than he'd ever seen them, and a pale pink blush dusted her cheeks. She had the look of a satisfied woman. Jealousy twisted in Archer's gut. What had she been doing in the Quarter? Was that what her protector was trying to hide? Did she have a lover?

A low growl erupted from him, and he resisted the urge to take her in his arms. To kiss her and lay his claim on her.

Mine, he thought.

He lowered himself in to the warm water and took her in to his arms. He guided them down to the shallower end of the pool where their feet could touch. He turned her so that her body was against the side of the pool.

"You're mine," he said.

Her eyes narrowed, her blue eyes shining like diamonds in the moonlight.

She said nothing.

He lowered his mouth to hers, softly kissing her at first. Enjoying the soft feel of her against his lips, his body. It wasn't enough. He had to have her. All of her. He wanted to consume her. He deepened the kiss. Her hands came up to entwine in his hair, pulling it softly.

One hand in her hair, his other hand trailed lower, sliding down her wet skin until his hand covered her breast. When his hand slid in to her bikini top, she moaned. He cupped her breast in one hand, squeezing the nipple between his fingers.

Josey's head shot back, another moan escaping from her lips.

Still exploring and tasting her mouth, he reached around and undid the tie that held her bikini top up. He pulled it off and threw it up beside his own clothes.

Using both hands now, one hand continued to caress her breast and the other hand traveled down to that part of her that was straining and rubbing against him.

"Feel good?" he asked as his hand slipped between her legs.

"Yesss." It was a hiss.

Teasing her, he rubbed slowly on top of the bikini bottom. She pushed in to his hand.

"More," she moaned.

"Not yet, baby."

He rubbed slowly still, stopping to run a teasing finger just underneath the fabric.

He raised his head to look at her. Her black hair was wet and floated out around her shoulders. Her eyes were closed. Her lips were red and swollen. She took his breath away, and he fought for control. All he wanted right then was to slide both of their bottoms down and drive himself far in to her.

He prayed she wouldn't say please. That word would be his undoing.

He took her mouth with his again, and guided her down in to the even shallower end of the pool. Near the steps. Now, he was able to take her breast in to his mouth. She gasped as he sucked on a nipple, sliding a finger in to her bikini bottom at the same time.

She went wild then, her body jerking toward him. Their kisses were so crazy they were almost bites.

He shoved his hand in to her bikini bottom and rubbed her warmth slowly. Her hips moved with the rhythm. He shuddered, trying to keep it together.

"Please, Archer," she whispered.

He lifted her up, and slid inside her. It was his turn to moan.

Her arms and legs wrapped around him as he drove in to her, moving slowly at first. Then his pace quickened. The soft sounds of the water splashing around as they moved mingled in with their moans.

"Archer!" she exclaimed, shuddering. As she tightened around him in release, he lost himself, too.

"Josephine!" He shouted her name as he lost himself.

They were silent as their heartbeats slowed down, still joined together. Archer was still throbbing.

"You will stay with me tonight?" she asked.

"Oh yeah, baby. I'm not finished with you. That was just the beginning."

He lowered his mouth to hers, kissing her swollen lips. "I won't be finished with you for a long, long time."

Alcide

ALCIDE SIPPED HIS DRINK, staring in to its depths as if looking for some kind of answer.

"There's nothing you can do, you know," Ivy said. "We've seen this happen again and again with those two." She poured a glass of wine for herself, and joined him on the other side of the now empty bar.

"They're together right now, you know," he said. "I can feel it."

He took another drink, draining the glass. He poured another drink from the bottle Ivy had opened and put beside him when he had sat down. "Half of me wants to go make him leave. Half of me wants to let it play out."

"Alcide, this might be a good thing."

"Lucy said the same thing."

"That shady bitch?" Ivy said with a smile. "She's probably right."

Alcide sighed heavily and pulled a cigarette out of the silver case in his breast pocket. He tapped in a few times and slid it between his lips.

"Alcide," Ivy started.

"I know. I know. Foolish law, if you ask me," he said, standing up. "I'll be back momentarily."

As he walked out, he heard Ivy mutter, "What are we going to do with them, Tobias?"

The vibration of the mug on the bar was the only response.

CHAPTER
Eight

Josey

JOSEY STRETCHED LAZILY, loving the exquisite soreness in parts she hadn't felt in a long, long time.

She looked over at Archer's sleeping form. He was lying on his back, sheets twisted around his waist. One arm fell across his head. Josey rolled up on to her side and resisted the urge to touch him. Just to make sure he was really there. To reassure herself that last night had really happened.

Her heart fluttered then, and not in a good way. Last night's endeavors had depleted her energy. They had made love until dawn, and it had taken its toll on her resources. She was hungry. She would need to feed again soon.

She slid out of bed and away from the temptation that was naked Archer. She pulled on her robe and walked quietly in to the kitchen to make coffee.

As she was pouring a cup, out of the corner of her eye, she saw a flash of red.

Lucy materialized in the kitchen, taking a seat at the bar. She was smiling lasciviously.

"You got lucky?"

"Good morning, Lucy," Josey said with a smile, raising

the coffee cup. "And, tell me, how exactly did Archer come to have the key to the rooftop gate and find his way up there?"

Lucy blinked a few times and grinned again. "Maybe he had some help."

"I see."

"Well, aren't you going to thank me?" Lucy pulled out a red and black lacy fan and waved it front of her face as if overheated.

Josey took a sip of the coffee before responding. "I don't know yet, Lucy. I had decided to stay away from him." Josey lowered her voice to a whisper. "He doesn't remember anything about who he was. Or what I am."

"Just tell him. Or let him figure it out on his own. That's what he did before."

"Vampires were a little more believable back then. There wasn't all this science."

"Why can't you enjoy this for now, Miss Josey? How many times in the past did you ask for just one more day with him? You've got it now."

A low moan distracted them then, and Josey rushed in to the bedroom. Archer lay on the bed, his head thrashing back and forth.

His breath was coming in shallow gasps. Josey started to reach out for him. When she saw the blood dripping from his nose, she jumped back in horror. Not at the sight of the blood, but at the beating of her heart as the brassy smell reached her senses and fired up her insides.

She gulped. "Get Alcide."

Lucy disappeared as Josey continued to back away, only stopping when her back bumped against the dresser. Frozen, she watched as Archer continued to toss and turn on the bed. *Why won't he wake up?* she thought.

Small drops of blood continued to seep out on to the white sheet. Josey held her hand over her nose to minimize the scent. Her heart still beat furiously, as if screaming out for the liquid that would sustain it.

Her door flew open, and, soon, Alcide's tall form filled the bedroom.

"Go now to my suite," he said, pointing to the door. "I've activated the shutters already. You will be safe there."

Josey looked at Archer again, red tears running down her face. "Did I do this?"

"Josephine, I feel your hunger. You cannot be here. Go now! I will meet you there. I will take care of this. I promise, *ma chère.*"

Josey listened that time, turning and fleeing from the room.

———

Archer

HIS HEAD POUNDED as a cold rag passed across his hot face, and Archer slowly opened his eyes. Expecting to see Josey after the night they had spent together, his eyes widened in shock when he saw Alcide by the bed.

For once, a smile crossed the man's face. "Not exactly who you were expecting, am I?"

He slowly shook his head. "Where is she?"

"An emergency. She had to step out for a moment." Alcide held up the rag in his hand, indicating the pink and red blood smears. "How long has this been going on?"

Archer bristled. "What business is it of yours?"

Those dark eyes narrowed. "Everything that happens to Josephine is my business."

"What is it with you two?"

"You wouldn't understand."

Archer longed for a cigarette, but had left them in his room. Alcide reached in to his breast pocket and pulled out a silver cigarette holder.

"I doubt they are to your taste, but they should work."

Archer nodded and took the offered cigarette and lighter. As he moved to sit, Alcide grabbed a robe out of the closet and threw it on the bed beside Archer. He lit a cigarette of his own and stared out the French doors while Archer tugged the soft fabric around him.

Alcide took a deep inhale of the cigarette and blew out the smoke. "There are things here in this hotel, in this town, that you would not understand. I will not attempt to explain. Be advised that Josephine's well-being is something that I take very seriously. I will do everything in my power to make sure she is safe."

He reached in to his pocket again and pulled out a room key. "I understand your key got misplaced last evening. Here is another. Your clothes are also at the foot of the bed. I trust that now that you are feeling better, you will be returning to your room."

"And Josey?"

"If Josey wants to see you, she knows where to find you."

"That's not good enough," Archer said. "What if I just want to wait here?"

"Then, you, sir, might be waiting a very long time."

"I can't believe that," Archer said.

Not after the night before. She wouldn't just walk away from him like that, would she? But what choice did he have at the moment? He couldn't just wait in her room for her to return like a stalker. He had no idea where she was.

Besides, he thought, he had a sound check coming up

later that afternoon. He exhaled a breath and stubbed out his cigarette in the ashtray Alcide provided.

He nodded to Alcide, and the big man smoothed his suit and tie. "I see we have an agreement."

With that, Alcide turned and left him alone in the room.

How in the hell had things gone so bad so quickly? Archer thought, then reached for his clothes. He reached up and touched his nose. Looking down, he saw the remnants of blood on his fingers. When had he started having nose bleeds?

———

Josey

"THAT'S EXACTLY why I can't 'just enjoy' it, Lucy! Did you see him? He was bleeding!" Josey said as she paced the floor of Alcide's living room. The dark surroundings of the gothic decor fit her mood. The candles flickering in black light fixtures on purple walls did little to illuminate the room. He had closed the shutters as he had said, and no sunlight seeped in to the room. It was as dark as night, and felt as such.

Lucy sat on the leather sofa, her head down. "I'm so sorry, Miss Josey. This is my fault. I really thought it would work."

"I have to stay away from him this time. We're only making it worse. I'm sure I caused this somehow. Sometimes, he looks at me and it's as if he's remembering something."

Thinking about the night before in the pool, Josey froze, her eyes wide.

"He called me Josephine," she whispered.

———

Alcide

THE FAMILIAR DING of the bell signaled Alcide's entrance in to *Enchantée*. He looked around at the objects in the store, frowning when he saw the old Victrola. He had brought that thing in here himself after it had shown up at the hotel. A gift for Josey from Archer delivered as his corpse laid out in the parlor.

"Hello, my child," Madame Vivian said as she entered the shop through the beaded curtain.

Alcide bowed his head. "Madame."

"You are troubled, *mon cher*."

"Deeply."

"Things are different this time, aren't they?"

"They are," Alcide commented, thinking of the way he'd found Archer that morning.

Madame Vivian fanned out the tarot cards in front of her. "I've laid out these cards many times over the last few days."

She pulled a single card out and showed it to Alcide.

He frowned.

"Every time, this card comes up."

The skeleton with the grim reaper scythe could only mean one thing. *La Morte.* The death card.

"One way or another, the cycle will end this time."

CHAPTER
Nine

Archer

AT THE CONCERT VENUE, Archer went through all the motions of the sound check as if he were on autopilot. It wasn't like he hadn't done it a thousand times before.

"What's wrong, man?" Neil, his lead guitarist, asked. "You seem distracted."

Distracted was an understatement. Archer was thirty-eight years old. He'd had his fair share of romances and even more one-night stands. He had lived up to the rocker persona in his early years on the road. Yet, no woman had made him feel like Josey did. Those eyes of hers stared right through him. Like she knew him. Had known him forever. And that dream he'd had that morning—that nightmare, really. Getting shot, seeing his own blood seep out of his chest. It had seemed so real.

He missed a chord, and the band turned to look at him.

"Sorry," he said, "I guess I spent too much time on Bourbon last night."

They smiled and nodded. *That* they understood. The thing with Josey, whatever it was, they never would. Archer Grayson *did not* lose his mind over a female. Ever.

"The show's tonight, man. You'd better get your head together. Drink some *Gatorade* or a Bloody Mary," Neil said, smiling.

Archer shuddered. "A Bloody Mary is the last thing I want right now." What he wanted was to get this sound check over with and get back to the hotel. To Josey.

———

Josey

DESPITE ALCIDE'S MISGIVINGS, Josey returned to her room. Would Archer return? Probably. Would she be ready? Yes. Alcide was already on the hunt in the Quarter to find someone suitable to satisfy her hunger. She could not be trusted in public the way she was at the moment. Luckily, New Orleans was full of people ready to have a good time. You just had to know where to look for them. Alcide would be back soon, she'd feed, and then figure out what she would do next.

Alcide had sent housekeeping to her room, so the bedroom was already swept clean of any residual scents of blood, and of the night before. The strong smell of bleach still lingered, turning her stomach. Still, she found herself sitting on his side of the bed, wondering what he had been dreaming about. Wishing things could have been different.

Josey ran her hand along the pillow that had cradled Archer's head just hours ago. She laid her head down on the same pillow, curled up into a ball, and sobbed.

———

Archer

ARCHER STEPPED out of the elevator and on to Josey's floor, envelope in hand. He had already stopped by the lounge and dropped tickets off for Ivy, the weird but fun bartender, and the couple who had recognized him the night before. Ivy had not arrived for work yet, but he left them anyway.

The rest of the sound check had gone well, and the band was pumped up and ready to go. Already, Archer could feel the endorphins begin to surge through his body. Whatever had plagued him that morning was gone. He didn't know what had called Josey away that morning, but he hoped she was back. And was ready for another round as much as he was.

He tapped on the door and listened. Nothing. He hadn't seen her downstairs. Where else would she be? He knocked again, a little louder.

"Josey?" he called, then listened.

No answer. He tried one more time before he sighed loudly. He leaned over and slipped the envelope under the door. As he was straightening, Alcide and a young man stepped out of the elevator. The young man didn't look like a hotel worker. He looked like someone who would hang out in some of the less reputable establishments in the French Quarter.

Spotting him, Alcide greeted him with the familiar frown. "Archer."

He raised an eyebrow. "Alcide."

Alcide neglected to introduce his companion. Stopping in front of Josey's door, he used his room key to open the door, bracing one big arm across the doorway as if to keep Archer from entering as the other man went inside.

"Josephine," he heard Alcide call as the door began to close, "we are here."

"What the hell?"

Where had she gone that morning? Why didn't she

answer the door when he called her name? Why was someone else going in there?

He ran a frustrated hand through his hair. He needed a drink. He'd go down to the lounge and see if Ivy had come on shift yet. Maybe he could get some answers out of her before he had to return to the concert hall.

CHAPTER
Ten

Archer

ARCHER SAT in the backstage area of the concert hall. The heavy drums and scream of electric guitar filtered in from the main stage. The opening band was local and good. *Epiphany* always tried to get local musicians to play for them. Their hunger and bright eyes always made him feel less jaded and more like the artist he was when he first started out. He seemed to feed off their energy and enthusiasm. Maybe someday he'd follow his dream of opening his own record label when the road got to be too hard. Rock stars and athletes had one thing in common. Most had a shelf life, and if you didn't watch it, you'd end up going from playing arenas full of fans, to small casino stages and cruises.

He sipped his whiskey. Would Josey come tonight? He still hadn't seen her. Alcide had stared at him as he walked through the hotel lobby earlier on his way to the theater. Archer had met that stare, tired of the man trying to intimidate him.

"What's up, man?" his bassist asked. "You're quiet tonight."

"Going through the set list again in my head. I think we made the right choice changing around the encore."

They had moved one of their more haunting songs to the end of the set. The melody was based on a weird dream he'd had about bootleggers. The old vibe and rhythm had become a favorite of theirs and the fans.

There was a knock on the door. "*Epiphany*, the band is finishing up. You guys are up as soon as we change out the stage."

"Thank you."

Archer nodded to his bassist. "Here we go."

He grabbed a cigarette and walked to the door that led outside. Every singer had their pre-show routine. Some did shots, some smoked a joint, some had sex, some did a line or two of coke.

Archer's routine was to go outside. He smoked a cigarette, stared up in to the night, and enjoyed a few moments of peace before the craziness of the hour and a half of an all-out rock and roll show. He'd be sore afterward, his muscles pushed to the breaking point. He'd be drenched in sweat, and the ring of applause would carry on in his head until he drifted off to sleep that night. The adrenaline would pump through his veins for hours after the show. He'd be lucky if he drifted off around dawn. He blew out a last puff from the cigarette. He'd be even luckier if he was in bed with Josey at dawn. If she showed.

———

Josey

JOSEY RIFLED through the clothes in her closet. *What did one wear to a rock concert?* She had no idea. She hadn't been to a real concert since the twenties, she recalled as she pushed the white fringed flapper dress aside.

Those had been the days, she thought. The decadence, the parties, the complete lack of inhibition. She had met Archer for the second time then, at a party in a speakeasy in the Quarter. He had lit her long, filtered cigarette. One look and they were both lost. She had fallen in to his arms that night, and hadn't left until he died in hers.

She shook her head. No use in dredging up old memories.

She smelled the clove smoke before she heard Alcide's presence.

"We're really doing this, then?" he asked.

She turned to look at him. He was reclining against her bar, cigarette resting loosely in one hand.

"You look like a gangster," she said, noting his suit and hat. "You been watching those old mob movies again?"

She eyed the flapper dress—maybe she would wear that one. They could go out in the Quarter like a famous gangster and his moll. A feathered headband fell from the closet shelf.

"Is that your vote too, Lucy?" Josey asked.

"It's a bad idea to wear that dress," Alcide said.

A white fur stole drifted down to the closet floor next, and Josey's mind was made up. She would dress up as a 1920s flapper. She wondered if she still had that old cigarette holder.

Bad idea be damned. Sometimes you had to live a little. She grinned at that old cliché; she hadn't technically lived in over two hundred years.

As she dressed, Alcide let out one of his long-suffering sighs. "I'm not even going to say I told you so this time."

"He's leaving soon and this will be over, Alcide. Let me have this one night."

Josey felt refreshed after her feeding. She had nearly lost

all control when Archer had banged on her door earlier that day. She had shut her bedroom door to filter the noise, and the scent of him. Luckily, Alcide had shown up when he had. She would go to the concert tonight, the temptation of seeing him perform too much to stand.

Alcide shook his head again, his eyes dark and sad.

Josey smiled and patted his arm. "It will be okay. I promise." She tugged on his arm, adding, "C'mon. Let's go."

Ivy met them in the lobby.

"Well, isn't this like old times…" Ivy said, eyeing their costumes. Not one to be outdone, she had decided to dress up as well.

Josey's lips twitched as she looked at Ivy's outrageous slinky red dress, shiny red lips, and visible vampire teeth.

"Really?" she asked Ivy, who only shrugged and smiled.

"If the teeth fit."

Josey had decided to wear the flapper costume after all. The once pristine white dress had now yellowed. In an antique store, the dress would cost a pretty penny, and had cost one back then. Crystal beads gleamed and sparkled in the light. A headband with a big white feather topped the outfit off, and Josey wore a bright shade of red lipstick.

"Shall we go?" Alcide said with a tip of his hat. He offered his arm to both women, and they walked through the lobby and out on to the street, catching the attention of more than one bystander.

———

THE CAR SLID to a stop in front of the theater. Alcide left his seat to open the door for Josey and Ivy. As he helped them out of the car, Josey heard the whispers. People wondering who they were. Asking each other if they were celebrities.

She walked through the crowd with her head held high, just as she had in the 20s. She wondered what might have changed since she was there the last time. Other than Archer not being by her side.

Her smile faltered for a moment, and she wondered if Alcide was right. Was wearing that outfit and going back to that theater a mistake?

Of course it was.

She looked over at Alcide, and he raised a dark eyebrow at her, giving her his best 'I told you so' look. He may not have verbalized it, but after all their time together, he knew how to get his point across.

"Look at all this. Isn't it delightfully vulgar?" Ivy gestured to the Halloween decorations. Skeletons wrapped in fake cobwebs were adorned in black and orange Carnival beads and top hats. The party never stopped in New Orleans. Not even when you were dead.

Alcide presented their tickets and led the way through the crowd that had already formed. His size and the sense of menace that emanated from him was a good crowd deterrent. People tended to give him a wide berth, and Josey and Ivy followed him through the crowd, up to their reserved balcony.

As they walked to their seats, Josey took in the surroundings. The lobby was classic and elegant. A crystal chandelier hung from the high ceiling, and white on white wallpaper with a floral motif adorned the walls. It was much like it had been the last time she was there.

Josey took her seat next to Alcide, as Ivy sat on his other side. A band was already playing. The loud and abrasive music was a little much for her taste, but their enthusiasm was entertaining. She wondered if Archer performed with that much passion.

Of course he did. That was how he lived his life. All of them.

She looked down at the crowd that surrounded the stage, wanting to get her mind off Archer. Mostly young people, but then everyone was young to her. She could smell the excitement and alcohol in their blood, and her fangs pounded again. Maybe she would feed again tonight.

She could always leave Alcide to sit with Ivy while Josey went and powdered her nose, and grabbed a quick snack.

"Thank you! Thank you very much! You've been a great crowd tonight!" the lead singer was saying. "Now, let's hear it for *Epiphany*!"

The crowd went wild. Fists went up in the air. The stage went dark.

Stagehands made quick work of the musical equipment on the stage. One set of drums disappeared and another, larger set appeared. A large black banner with the word *Epiphany* in big white letters dropped down behind the drum set.

It was all quite fascinating.

A man stepped out with a microphone as the band members began to take their places on the stage.

"Are you guys ready for *Epiphany*?" he yelled.

The crowd screamed.

"I can't hear you!" he said.

The crowd went even more insane.

"Ladies and gentlemen, *Eternal Productions* is pleased to bring you *Epiphany*!"

The theater went dark, and the music began. The drums, the guitar, the bass, it was all so loud, Josey could feel it in her gut. It was quite sensual, really. Primitive. Josey understood the allure.

Where was Archer?

The spotlight shot on, and there he was in the middle of the stage. His mic in hand, he belted out the lyrics to a song that the crowd knew instantly, singing along with him. Ivy included.

Guitar strapped around his chest, he played along.

He really had an incredible singing voice. Deep and throaty. Strong. That was new.

As the concert went on, his lyrics spoke of love and loss. Of overcoming difficulties. Anthems for the broken. Old soul songs. And although he didn't realize it, Archer had a very old soul.

His eyes scanned the crowd. The balcony first. His lips curved in a sensual smile when he saw her there. A little shiver shot through her. She'd made her mind up earlier. She would have her way with him. Erase his memory and let him leave when his stay was over.

———

ALMOST TWO HOURS LATER, the lights went out and Josey stood to leave. "No, Josey. It's not over yet," Ivy said.

Josey gestured to the dark stage. "But they said thank you and the lights went out."

"They'll do an encore," Ivy said.

"Oh?"

"Yes."

"Interesting."

Sure enough, the band was back out, instruments back in hand. Archer again took his place front and center and began to sing.

They sang two more songs, and then started playing a third one.

The melody was the same song she and Archer had heard in that very theatre.

Josey came out of her seat. Her hands gripped the balcony railing.

————

Archer

ARCHER'S EYES MET HERS, and his reaction was as visceral as her own. He felt as if he'd been shot in the chest. The pain was so intense, he swore his heart stopped for a moment. Years of performing saved him from an embarrassing fumble as habit kept his fingers strumming and the lyrics coming out. Even if he did sound a bit breathless, most would blame it on the long, grueling performance. Fear kept him from looking up again at Josey. What was wrong with him?

His heart pounded as he sang the last few haunting notes of the song. He threw a guitar pick in to the audience and took a final bow with the band.

Thankfully, he ended all his performances with the same routine as he started them, and, soon, he was walking through the back door, ready to feel the cool air of the October night and for the quiet to settle his thoughts and his nerves.

He leaned against the brick wall and closed his eyes, willing himself to breathe. His heart had been beating erratically since he'd seen Josey.

As he closed his eyes, he pictured her in that white dress. That red lipstick. He felt like he had seen it before.

He could almost see himself in a 1920s style suit, a fedora topping his head. Josey came down the winding stairs of the hotel. His blood raced as he saw her in that dress, her white legs peeking out from under that short skirt. Her black hair was curled tightly, and her head was adorned with a jeweled and feathered headband.

SHE MET him at the foot of the stairs, and Archer gathered her in to his arms and kissed her solidly. She pressed her body up against his. His hands were about to slide from her waist to her backside when she giggled huskily.

"Careful, dear. We're going to put on a show. I know this is N'awlins and all, but I'd prefer to not have customers and employees wagging their tongues about me."

"As you wish, my dear," he said. He dropped his hand reluctantly. Offering his arm, he asked, "Shall we go?"

"HELLO, ARCHER."

Archer's eyes popped open, and there she was in front of him, looking just like his vision.

"Josey."

"I can't help myself," she said. "I'm so sorry."

"For what?" was on the tip of his tongue, but he found his tongue otherwise occupied as she shoved him against the wall with a force that seemed almost unnatural.

That time, she was the aggressor. Her hands flew to his hair, her hands cold against his overheated skin. The shock aroused him further.

His hands slid up her slim hips, and he wrapped his hands around her waist, holding her there. She wasn't going anywhere.

She caught his bottom lip between her teeth, and Archer felt the blood completely rush from his head to other regions of his body.

His hands slipped from her waist, up her back to cradle her neck to encourage her to go deeper. To devour him.

The door to the outside opened. "Mr. Grayson? Oh, oh. I'm so sorry."

"What?" he asked more sharply than he intended, his frustration running heavy through his body.

"They're ready for you in the VIP section."

"Damn it! This isn't over," he said, looking at Josey, who looked beautiful in the moonlight. Her lips were smudged and shiny; the red almost looked like blood. Her hair was in disarray and her clothes were slightly disheveled. He wanted her to look like that again. Soon.

She nodded, then said, "You will meet me in my room at the hotel an hour before sunrise."

Archer reached out and caressed her cheek. "I'll be there."

She turned and all but disappeared in to the alley.

He followed his manager, Mike, in to the building.

"Archer, it was a good crowd tonight," Mike was saying, but Archer was only halfway listening, his mind still on what had happened in the alley and what was to come.

When they stopped unexpectedly in the hall, Archer turned to look at the man curiously.

"Dude," Mike said, "you probably should…" He made a swiping motion with his hand to his mouth. "Did she bite your lip or something? She's taking this Halloween vibe too far."

Archer ran the back of his hand across his throbbing mouth. Sure enough, there was a red stain on his hand as he pulled it back and looked at it. That kiss had been intense. He hadn't even realized. *Tonight is going to be interesting*, he thought, and followed his manager to the VIP section to greet his fans.

Josey

JOSEY TOOK a moment in the dark alley after disappearing from Archer to compose herself. She could not go back to Alcide and Ivy in her overheated and aroused state. She licked her lips, and she could still taste Archer's blood in her mouth. It tasted like it always did, smoky and dark, like chocolate and whiskey. Intoxicating.

She frowned a little at the taste of something else. Something different and dark.

She shook off the feeling. She was going to enjoy tonight. She was going to leave him spent and empty, erase his memory, and let him go. It was the only thing she could do. She could not see him die again.

Unless…

"Don't," Alcide said, suddenly beside her. "Don't even think about it. You would pull him from his life like you were taken? You were lying in that hospital bed, ready to die, when she came to you and turned you. You hated her for how long? What if he hates you? What if he can't handle leaving his mortal life?"

"You're right, you know."

"Of course I am." He offered her the rare smile he reserved for her and his arm. "Let's go find our Ivy before she gets in to mischief."

CHAPTER
Eleven

Archer

ARCHER FINISHED up with the VIP group, made his comments to the reporters, and showered in the tour bus the band had arrived in. Stepping out in to the cool fall air, he shivered. He considered taking a cab to the hotel, but, sometimes, with French Quarter one-ways, foot traffic, and congestion in general, it would probably be quicker to walk to the hotel. Plus, the exercise would allow him to work off the show adrenaline. He could be nice and calm when he got to Josey. He could take it nice and slow.

He walked through the streets, careful to keep to the main routes and around crowds. He wasn't scared, but New Orleans wasn't on the list of high crime areas for no reason.

Josephine, he thought. He could see her again in the moonlight in the alley. That feather. Those lips. His head pounded again, and he nearly swooned. What was wrong with him? He reached out and put his hand on the closest building for support until the dizziness passed.

After a moment, his head cleared and he started walking again, turning on Royal toward the hotel.

Soft music played in the distance, but not the normal Quarter music. It was the song he'd been hearing at the hotel and in his dreams.

"*Dream a little dream of me…*"

As if in a trance, he followed the sounds of old jazz and trumpets to its source.

Enchantée. The weird store with the interesting old lady.

The door was already open, and Archer walked in. Madame Vivian was there, standing behind the counter just as she was the last time he'd been there.

"Good evening, Mr. Grayson. Have you come for your reading? I have answers you seek."

He smiled and shook his head. "Not tonight. I have places I need to be. I still want that old Victrola, though. Are you ready to part with it yet?"

"I told you that it isn't for sale."

"I guess that's it, then," he said, turning to leave.

He was almost to the door when she spoke again, her words stopping him in his tracks.

"I know why you are having the dreams you're having."

He turned again to face her, not saying anything.

"I know the pain you feel," she pointed at her chest, "right here. It feels like a gunshot, doesn't it? I know about the visions. The headaches. The nosebleed."

"How do you know all that?"

She smiled then. "I know a lot of things. I've been around a long time, Mr. Grayson. That's not the important part."

"What is, then?"

"I can make you remember. You're seeing things in your dreams, aren't you?"

Archer was still skeptical.

With a flick of her wrist, the music stopped and the shop fell silent.

75

Okay. That was weird, he thought. Another flick, and the music came back on. Only louder. The lights flickered, and his head began to pound.

He looked at Madame Vivian again, and another flash of a vision came to him. He'd been there before.

"Yes. Yes you have." She nodded. "Come see, my child. It is time."

HE FOLLOWED her in to the back room, and his eyes widened at the various candles, dolls, and glass jars filled with different colors of liquid.

His eyes darted to the door. *This was a bad, bad idea*.

"You are safe here. I seek only to help," she said as she gestured to the seat at the small table. "Please sit."

He looked in to her crystal blue eyes and sat.

She took a bottle of clear liquid and sprinkled it in a circle around the table.

"Think, my child. Close your eyes and think back. Think back and remember." She lit a white candle and placed it in the middle of the table. She then said a few words in a language Archer didn't understand, and blew out the candle.

Archer jerked as the memories flooded his mind. He felt the playing cards in his hands as he gambled on the riverboat, then the warm water surrounding him after the boat sank in to the dark Mississippi. Then, the panic as the water overtook him.

His heart pounded as he remembered meeting Josey in the speakeasy on a bootlegging mission. Her smile. Next was her baring her teeth to him, showing him what she really was. His fear and excitement as she had slid those fangs in to his neck the first time. The night they'd gone to the theater. The same venue he'd played that very evening. Then the pain in his chest as he'd been shot on the run that had gone bad.

With a deep gulp of breath, he opened his eyes.

"This can't be true."

"It is, my child. Go to Josey."

He stood up on shaky legs.

"That feeling will pass soon. Wait a moment to regain your strength. The Quarter is no place to wander around in your condition. There is one more thing, my child."

"What is it?"

"Those headaches. The nosebleeds. Those are only going to get worse. You are dying, my child. There is something growing in your brain. You can go to a modern doctor and he will tell you the same. He will want to put you through treatments. And you can, if you want. However, if you do not, you will not make it. If you choose the second, you will still have options."

"Options?"

"You will see." She smiled and patted his hand. "For now, go see your woman. She grows impatient waiting for you."

He smiled. Whatever weirdness had gone on in the little shop, there was something normal at the end of the tunnel. He got up and nodded at the old woman.

"Good evening, Madame Vivian."

"Good evening, *mon cher*. And come back to see me."

"I will."

"I know you will."

Archer smiled at her one more time and ducked out through the beaded curtain. It was time for more answers.

————

Josey

JOSEY STOOD on the balcony of her quarters. She looked down at the dimly lit area around the bubbling fountain. She took in the year-round greenery that surrounded the stone water feature, and the various night blooming flowers she'd always kept after she had been changed.

She turned as the antique clock chimed. Archer should be knocking anytime. Josey could already see the slight turning of the night sky. She closed the French doors and activated the shutters that would keep out the sun's dangerous light.

Her heart beat in anticipation as she looked at the door again. Would he come?

A cool breeze wafted through the room, and Josey looked over to the bed. Lucy materialized, perching on the blue bedspread.

"He's going to come, you know."

"I know."

"It's going to be different this time."

"I hope so, Lucy. I hope so. He doesn't even remember his former lives with me."

"That's good. A fresh start." Lucy frowned. "We don't always get those."

Josey nodded. "I know."

A heavy knock sounded at the door. Archer was there.

Josey glanced at Lucy, who winked before she disappeared. Josey inhaled a deep breath, already smelling Archer's scent, and sensing the need that pounded through his veins. She ran her lips across the tops of her fangs and smiled.

She padded silently across the hardwood floor, then opened the door.

Archer was, indeed, there. His brown eyes were dark with desire already. He walked across the threshold. His hands circled her waist, and Josey allowed herself to be backed up against the wall.

Reaching up, he gently pressed her head back. One finger came up to her lips. He traced lips that covered her pounding fangs. Closing her eyes, she sighed. She would never get through the night without feeding on him.

"Josephine." His voice was ragged.

"Yes?"

He tilted his head to the side, exposing thick neck muscles. Josey fought for control.

"Madame Vivian. She was right. I know what you are. I remember. I remember everything."

Shocked, she opened her eyes and looked in to his. He knew. He crooked his head to the side as his vein throbbed. Josey licked her lips. Talking could wait. They had a lifetime or more to talk.

"This time, you're mine forever," she said, then sank her fangs deep in to his neck.

Hard Hearted Hannah

#2 IN SERIES

CHAPTER
One

"OVER MY DEAD BODY!" Hannah Montgomery's voice rang out through the small office of the Charleston lifestyle magazine, 843. As always, her words aimed to draw blood. His blood.

Like it's not already. He didn't think the woman had a heart, one that beat and pumped blood anyway.

Considering they were both in a meeting with the Ice Queen's father, he thought it best to keep his mouth shut. He wasn't any happier about the new travel arrangements than she. However, since it was her father, she could speak her mind.

"You aren't going to New Orleans by yourself," Jack said to Hannah. "It's not safe. Someone got shot in the Quarter just last week. I'd feel so much better if you went with someone. Humor your father. I have enough gray hair. I'd go but I don't think that's what you want either." Her dad smiled.

"But with him?"

"I don't have the plague, you know. You don't have to say it like that," Julien said.

"He doesn't have the plague," Jack repeated, "and it's settled. You can go alone to New Orleans for Voodoo Fest. But Julien is going too."

Julien contained the deep sigh that wanted to escape. When he and Jack talked about this project a few weeks ago, he'd been so excited. Being from Louisiana, he'd jumped at the chance to go back.

Until Hannah had been included. He had no idea she even wanted to go on this trip. He had no idea she liked anything except making him feel like a piece of trash discarded on Bourbon Street. Now, he was stuck with her. He had worked for Jack long enough to know that there would be no convincing the man otherwise.

If Julien wanted this gig in New Orleans, he'd have to deal with Hannah. Julien never turned down a job. Come hell, high water, or freezing rain, he was going to New Orleans.

———

JULIEN PLACED the rest of his photography equipment in the trunk and slammed it shut.

This is going to be a long trip, he thought to himself again. The nine-hour drive from Savannah to New Orleans would feel like a lifetime cooped up in the car with her.

Hannah Montgomery, the boss's daughter. Since she moved back from California, the woman had been intolerable. She was snippy, dismissive, and just an overall bitch.

Julien had worked for Hannah's dad since he'd started doing photography right out of college. He could remember when she hadn't been so awful. She'd once had an easy smile and a contagious laugh. What happened since then? Julien had no clue. She damn sure wasn't sharing her reasons, either.

They usually didn't travel together. Hannah rarely went out on location, but, apparently, one of her favorite bands, Epiphany, was playing at Voodoo Festival. Julien was going there to photograph the festival and New Orleans during Halloween for the magazine. When her father found out they were going at the same time, he'd insisted they travel together. The impossible woman e-mailed him an itinerary, planning out each day's activities by the hour. People didn't plan out trips in NOLA. Being from South Louisiana, Julien had been to the city many times. You went with a simple agenda in mind, and you rolled with the flow.

This is going to be a long trip.

Hard Hearted Hannah
Available Now:
http://a.co/ehYwczD

ABOUT THE
Author

Jolie St. Amant

She fell in love with all things New Orleans after reading
Interview with the Vampire by Anne Rice. Now, a frequent
visitor to the Crescent City, she can often be found getting
inspiration from ghost tours or sipping *cafe au lait* at Cafe
du Monde.

Facebook:
https://www.facebook.com/JolieStAmant/

Twitter:
https://twitter.com/JolieStAmant

Made in the USA
Columbia, SC
14 May 2018